The Bowl
of Fruit

Joyce Dunbar

illustrated by

Helen Craig

CANDLEWICK PRESS
CAMBRIDGE, MASSACHUSETTS

Panda and Gander

had a big bowl of

fruit to share.

Panda took a pear.

Gander took a pomegranate.

"I like pears,"

said Panda.

"And I like pomegranates,"

said Gander.

"I like the way you can eat a pear,"
said Panda. "You can pull off the
stem and eat it from the top."

"And I like the way you can eat
a pomegranate," said Gander.
"You can cut it in half and pick
out the seeds."

Panda pulled the stem off his pear
and ate it from the top.
"All gone," said Panda.

Gander cut his pomegranate
in half and picked out the seeds.
"Pomegranates are full of seeds,"
said Gander.

Panda took a banana.

"I like the way you can eat a banana," said Panda. "You pull down the peel so that it looks like wings."

"All gone," said Panda.

"Pomegranates take a lot of picking," said Gander.

Panda took a tangerine.

"I like the way you can eat a tangerine," said Panda. "Slice by slice. Slice by slice is very nice."

"Seed by seed is very slow," said Gander.

"All gone," said Panda.

"Seedy and slow," said Gander.

Panda helped himself to an apple.

"I like the way you can eat an apple,"
said Panda. "Big crunchy bites
around the middle."

"All gone," said Panda.

Gander was still picking seeds.

"The red seeds are very sweet.

The yellow pith is very bitter."

Panda took some grapes.
"I like the way you can eat grapes,"
said Panda. "You bite them off,
one at a time."

"All gone," said Panda.
"I am putting all the seeds in a pile,"
said Gander.
"So you are," said Panda.

"There's a pile of peel. There's a pile of pith. There's a pile of seeds," said Gander.

"Juicy red seeds," said Panda.

"That's right," said Gander.

"Juicy red seeds without pith," said Panda.

"That's right," said Gander.

"When I have put all the seeds in

a pile I will eat them all in one bite,"

said Gander.

"Will you?" said Panda.

"Yes," said Gander. "And see, I have

almost finished. Look, what a big

pile of pomegranate seeds."

"Gander," said Panda.

"What is it?" said Gander.

"There are some cherries left
 in the fruit bowl."

"So there are," said Gander.

"There are enough cherries
to share," said Panda.

"So there are," said Gander.

"I like what you can do with cherries," said Panda. "You can dangle them over your ears."

"I don't have the right kind of ears," said Gander.

"Well, dangle them somewhere else,"
said Panda.

"All right, after I have eaten
my pomegranate seeds,"
said Gander.

Gander started to eat his
pomegranate seeds.

He scooped and he slurped and
he swallowed.

"What about me?" said Panda.

"What about you?" said Gander.

"I shared my cherries with you,

so you should share your

pomegranate seeds with me,"

said Panda.

"All right," said Gander.

"If you give me a share of the pear."

"It's all gone," said Panda.

"How about a share of the banana?"

"All gone," said Panda.

"How about a share of the tangerine?"

"That's all gone, too," said Panda.

"All right, how about the apple and
 the grapes?"

"All gone," said Panda.

"Well, you see these pomegranate seed

"Yes," said Panda.

"All gone!" said Gander. And he dangled the cherries on his boots.